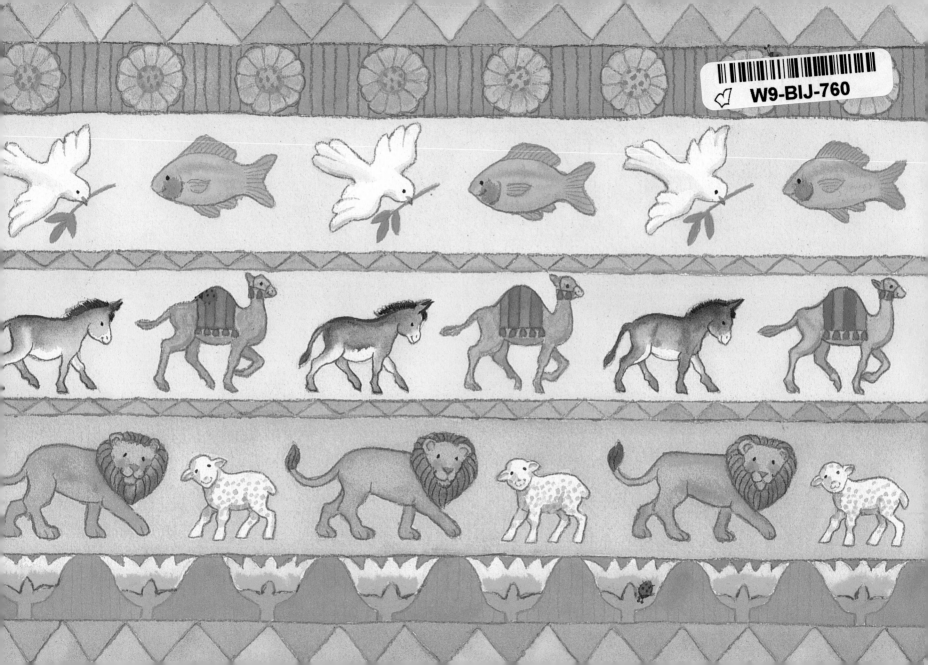

This book belongs to

GOOD NEWS
for little people

KENNETH N.
TAYLOR

Illustrated by
Nancy Munger

TYNDALE HOUSE PUBLISHERS, INC.   WHEATON, ILLINOIS

Other Children's Books by Kenneth N. Taylor

Big Thoughts for Little People
Giant Steps for Little People
Wise Words for Little People

My First Bible in Pictures
The Bible in Pictures for Little Eyes
The New Testament in Pictures for Little Eyes

Library of Congress Catalog Card Number 90-71452
ISBN 0-8423-6628-8
Printed in the United States of America
96 95 94 93 92 91
7   6   5   4   3   2   1

A PREFACE

(To be read by parents and grandparents)

Jesus loves me
This I know
For the Bible
Tells me so

This little song is filled with great truths. How important it is for even the smallest child to know that he or she is loved. And how wonderful to grow up knowing the love of Jesus.

How will the child learn about this beautiful fact? "The Bible tells me so." Yes, God has told us in the Bible about Jesus' love for little people—as well as for their parents and grandparents.

This book tells in simple language the stories about Jesus—how he walked on the water to rescue his friends, how he brought a twelve-year-old girl back to life, and how he healed many people who were sick. These are true stories every child needs to know. For at a very young age a child can learn not only that Jesus loves us but to love him in return.

That is the purpose of this book.

KENNETH N. TAYLOR

P.S. Don't forget to look for the ladybugs on many of the pages!

The angel came to Mary
With news of wondrous joy:
She was going to have a baby,
And he would be God's boy!

God sent this angel to Mary's house. The angel's name is Gabriel. He has come down from heaven to tell Mary some exciting news. The wonderful news is that Mary is going to have a baby, and the baby will be God's son! The angel tells Mary that the baby's name will be Jesus. The name *Jesus* has a special meaning. It means "Savior." It means that Jesus saves us. Now we can be God's friends. How wonderful that God sent Jesus to save us!

SOME QUESTIONS TO ANSWER
1. What is the angel's name?
2. What is the baby's name?
3. Who is Jesus' father?
4. Why did God send Jesus?

A LITTLE PRAYER
Dear Father in heaven, thank you for sending Jesus to save us.

A BIBLE VERSE FOR YOU TO SAY
His Kingdom shall never end! LUKE 1:33

The sheep and little lambs look up.
The sky is filled with light.
The angels sing to shepherds
Of Jesus' birth that night.

See the many, many angels! It was nighttime, and the men taking care of the sheep were very frightened. They had never seen angels before. But one of the angels told them, "Don't be afraid. We have come with wonderful news. Jesus was born tonight! He is the Savior! He is Christ, the Lord." The angels told the shepherds to go to the town of Bethlehem. They would find the baby Jesus with Mary and Joseph in a barn. The baby would be wrapped in a blanket. He would be lying in the hay in a manger, where the donkeys and cows eat their suppers. How happy the shepherds were to hear that their Savior was born!

SOME QUESTIONS TO ANSWER
1. Why were the men afraid at first?
2. What happy news did the angels bring?

A LITTLE PRAYER
Thank you, God, for your son, Jesus. Thank you that he is our Savior.

A BIBLE VERSE FOR YOU TO SAY
I bring you the most joyful news ever told! *The Savior has been born*

tonight in Bethlehem! LUKE 2:10-11

Away in a manger, No crib for a bed, The little Lord Jesus Laid down his sweet head.

The shepherds hurried to Bethlehem to find the baby, God's son. Now they have come to the barn where Jesus was born. They have found the baby Jesus, lying in a manger! The shepherds are worshiping Jesus. Before Jesus was born, he wasn't a baby. He lived with God in heaven. Jesus made the world and everything in it. But God asked him to become Mary's baby. The shepherds told everyone, "This baby, Jesus, is our Savior! The angels told us so!" And everyone was filled with joy and wonder because God's son was born.

SOME QUESTIONS TO ANSWER
1. Point to Jesus and to Mary.
2. Where was Jesus before he was born?

A LITTLE PRAYER
Dear Jesus, thank you for becoming a baby. Thank you for coming to save me.

A BIBLE VERSE FOR YOU TO SAY
God loved the world so much that he gave his only Son. JOHN 3:16

The wise men came from far away
To greet the newborn king.
They knelt before him and they said,
"Our gifts to you we bring."

These wise men have come a long way to find Jesus. They were far away when they learned that Jesus was born. So they got on their camels and rode and rode and rode. A star showed them where to go. The wise men finally came to Bethlehem. They found the house where Jesus lived with his mother, Mary, and with Joseph. When they saw the baby Jesus they were very glad. They got down on their knees in front of him to show how great Jesus is. Then they gave him many presents, because Jesus is the king.

SOME QUESTIONS TO ANSWER
1. How did the wise men know where to find Jesus?
2. Why did they give him presents?

A LITTLE PRAYER
Dear God, help me to know how great and good you are. Help me always to want to give you some of my good things.

A BIBLE VERSE FOR YOU TO SAY
The wise men threw themselves down before him, worshiping. MATTHEW

The grown-ups stood and listened
To the questions Jesus raised.
This boy had so much wisdom
That they were all amazed.

Now Jesus is twelve years old. Mary and Joseph and lots of other people went on a long walk to another city. They thought Jesus was walking with his friends. They didn't know Jesus had stayed behind. He went into God's house to talk to the important men there. Outside, Joseph and Mary were asking everyone, "Where is Jesus? Have you seen him anywhere?" Finally they found him! How happy they were! Jesus wondered why they didn't know where he was. "God's house is my Father's house," he told them. "Didn't you know I'd be here?" Then he went home with Mary and Joseph, and he always obeyed them.

SOME QUESTIONS TO ANSWER
1. Who was Jesus' mother?
2. Who is his Father?

A LITTLE PRAYER
Dear Father in heaven, thank you for your son, Jesus. Thank you that he is my friend.

A BIBLE VERSE FOR YOU TO SAY
So Jesus grew both tall and wise.   And he was loved by both God and

man. LUKE 2:52

Jesus calls his disciples—
At first a pair of brothers,
Then ten more men, and you, and me,
And many, many others.

Now Jesus has grown up and become a big man. He is asking two brothers to come with him. They can be his special friends and helpers. Soon he will find ten more men to be with him. He will teach them about God. He will show them how to love each other and everyone else. Jesus will give them power to do many wonderful things. These twelve friends of Jesus are called his disciples. Sometimes they are called his apostles. You and I can be Jesus' friends too. Our friend Jesus is here with us in this room, even though we can't see him. He has asked us to be his helpers. We will do whatever he says.

SOME QUESTIONS TO ANSWER
1. What are Jesus' special friends called?
2. Does Jesus want you to be his special friend?

A LITTLE PRAYER
Dear Jesus, thank you for asking me to be your special friend.

A BIBLE VERSE FOR YOU TO SAY
Jesus called out, "Come along with me!..." They left their nets at

once and went with him. MATTHEW 4:19-20

This little girl got sick and died, But Jesus came and said, "Get up, dear child, and run and play." Then she jumped out of bed!

This girl is happily talking to Jesus. Just a few minutes ago she was dead! One day she began to feel sick. She didn't want to play or even get out of bed. The doctor said she would die. Then her father heard that Jesus could help. He ran to find Jesus, and he asked Jesus to make his daughter well. Jesus came with him. But it was too late. The girl was already dead. She could not move at all. Jesus took her cold, stiff hand in his and said, "Get up, little girl!" And she jumped up and walked around! She wasn't dead anymore! Jesus made her alive again! Then Jesus said, "She's hungry. Give her something to eat!"

SOME QUESTIONS TO ANSWER
1. Why couldn't the girl move before Jesus came?
2. What did Jesus do?

A LITTLE PRAYER
Dear Jesus, thank you for making the girl alive after she was dead. Thank you for making her family happy again.

A BIBLE VERSE FOR YOU TO SAY
Taking her by the hand he said to her, "Get up, little girl!" And she

jumped up and walked around! MARK 5:41-42

He couldn't move his hands or feet,
He couldn't move at all.
Then Jesus said, "Get up and walk!"
He did, and didn't fall.

This man couldn't walk. His legs wouldn't hold him up. His friends said, "Jesus can help him. Jesus can make him well again. Let's take him to Jesus." So they carried him on a mat to the house where Jesus was preaching. But too many people were there. His friends could not carry him through all the people. "I have an idea," one of his friends said. "Let's make a hole in the roof. Let's gently lower him down right in front of Jesus!" Jesus looked up and saw the sick man's friends. Jesus knew they believed he would make the man well. So Jesus told the sick man to stand up and go home. The man jumped up and walked away! How wonderful Jesus is!

SOME QUESTIONS TO ANSWER
1. Why did the man's friends want to take him to Jesus?
2. What did Jesus tell the man to do?

A LITTLE PRAYER
Dear Jesus, thank you for making the man walk. Thank you for all the wonderful things you do.

A BIBLE VERSE FOR YOU TO SAY
He said to the man, "My friend,   your sins are forgiven!" LUKE 5:20

Jesus loves the little children,
All the children of the world.
Red and yellow, black and white,
They are precious in his sight.
Jesus loves the little children of the world.

One day some mothers brought their little children to Jesus. The mothers wanted Jesus to put his hand on the children's heads and bless them. But Jesus' friends told the mothers to take the children away. "Go away," they said. "Jesus doesn't have time to talk to children." But Jesus was not pleased with his friends for saying this. Jesus said, "Let the little children come to me. Don't ever say they can't." Then Jesus took the children in his arms and blessed them. Jesus loves little children very much. Don't ever forget that he loves you.

SOME QUESTIONS TO ANSWER
1. What did Jesus' friends say to the mothers?
2. What did Jesus say to his friends?
3. How does Jesus feel about you?

A LITTLE PRAYER
Thank you, God, for loving me. Thank you that Jesus doesn't say, "Go away." Thank you that I can come to Jesus so he can bless me.

A BIBLE VERSE FOR YOU TO SAY
Jesus said, "Let the little children come to me. Don't stop them."

MATTHEW 19:14

The man is blind, he cannot see. He cannot use his eyes. But Jesus came and made him well. What a wonderful surprise!

This man was blind. He couldn't see the road or the trees or the flowers or the people. Everything was dark, with no light at all. Close your eyes and walk across the room, and you can tell how he felt. Look at Jesus healing the blind man so he can see! Jesus can do things like this because he is God's son. He can do anything. How wonderful he is! You can see how happy the man is. He was blind and now he can see. He is jumping for joy! He can see all the pretty things, and he can see his friends. He never saw them before, because he was blind.

SOME QUESTIONS TO ANSWER
1. Why is the man so happy?
2. Do you think he thanked Jesus?
3. Have you ever thanked Jesus because you can see? Let's do it now.

A LITTLE PRAYER
Jesus, thank you because I can see the beautiful things you made. Thank you, thank you, thank you.

A BIBLE VERSE FOR YOU TO SAY
Jesus said, "All right, begin seeing! Your faith has healed you." LUKE

8:42

THE GOOD SAMARITAN

A man lay bleeding by the road.
Some people passed him by.
But one man stopped and helped him up
And didn't let him die.

This man was attacked by robbers. They beat him up until he was half-dead. Then they took his money and his donkey, and they ran away. One man saw him lying there, but he walked on by. He didn't want to be bothered. Someone else went over and looked at the hurt man, but he didn't help him either. The third man did the right thing. He helped! He put medicine and bandages on the hurt man's wounds. He will take the hurt man to a place where he can get better. The kind man is called the Good Samaritan. Jesus wants us to be Good Samaritans too by helping people.

SOME QUESTIONS TO ANSWER
1. What did the first man do for the hurt man?
2. What did the second man do?
3. What did the Good Samaritan do?
4. Can you help somebody today?

A LITTLE PRAYER
Dear Father in heaven, thank you that the Good Samaritan helped the man who was hurt. Help me to be a helper too.

A BIBLE VERSE FOR YOU TO SAY
When he saw the man, he felt deep pity. LUKE 10:33

JESUS FEEDS FIVE THOUSAND

A little boy had brought his lunch—
Two fish, five loaves of bread.
In Jesus' hands it grew until
The hungry crowd was fed.

This boy's mother gave him a picnic lunch. She gave him five small loaves of bread and two fish. He went with a big crowd of people to listen to Jesus. When it was mealtime, do you know what? No one else had any food! And all the people were hungry. One of Jesus' friends asked the boy if he would give his food to Jesus. "Yes," he said, "of course I will." Jesus broke the bread and fish into pieces. He gave them to his disciples to give to the people. Then a wonderful miracle happened. Jesus made the boy's small lunch become enough food for five thousand people! They ate and ate and ate until they were full. And there was a lot left over!

SOME QUESTIONS TO ANSWER
1. What did Jesus do with the five loaves and two fish?
2. How many people were hungry after Jesus fed them?

A LITTLE PRAYER
Thank you, God, for giving Jesus the power to make the bread and fish become enough for everyone.

A BIBLE VERSE FOR YOU TO SAY
He gives food to the hungry. PSALM 146:7

Jesus' friend named Lazarus Got very sick and died. But Jesus came and called to him— And then he came to life.

What is happening in this picture? Something wonderful and strange. The man wrapped up in strips of cloth is Jesus' friend Lazarus. He was very sick, and four days ago he died. His body was put inside a hole in the rock. Have you ever seen a dead bird, or fish, or little animal? Something dead can never move again. But Lazarus died, and here he is alive again! How did this happen? Jesus did it! Jesus came and called to Lazarus. If you or I called to Lazarus, he could not have heard us because he was dead. But when Jesus called, Lazarus heard him and came out. What wonderful power Jesus has! He can make dead people alive again! Now Lazarus's friends will unwrap him so he can go home.

SOME QUESTIONS TO ANSWER
1. Why was Lazarus in the hole in the rock?
2. How did he become alive again?

A LITTLE PRAYER
Thank you, God, for making Lazarus alive and well again.
Thank you for your great power.

A BIBLE VERSE FOR YOU TO SAY
He shouted, "Lazarus, come out!" And Lazarus came out! JOHN 11:43-4

Who can walk on water?
It just cannot be done!
But Jesus did it easily—
He is the only one.

Very early one morning, Jesus' friends were in a boat on a lake.
They were rowing hard against the wind. Jesus wasn't there to
help them. Jesus walked out from the beach to be with them.
Look! He is walking on top of the water! His friends in the boat
are frightened. They have never seen anyone walk on water.
They think Jesus is a ghost! Jesus calls out to them, "It is I.
Don't be afraid." Then they are excited and happy, and Jesus
gets into the boat with them.

SOME QUESTIONS TO ANSWER
1. Did Jesus swim out to the boat?
2. Can you walk on water?
3. Who walked on the water?

A LITTLE PRAYER
Thank you, God, for the wonderful things Jesus can do. Thank
you that he will use his great power to help me.

A BIBLE VERSE FOR YOU TO SAY
"It's all right," he said. *"It is I! Don't be afraid."* MARK 6:50

JESUS MAKES ALL THE PEOPLE WELL

The people came from all around—
All weak and sick and sad.
But Jesus' touch has made them well.
They're thankful now, and glad!

Look at all the people watching Jesus! They are excited about what he is doing. He is making sick people well! Can you see all the sick people? Some are on crutches because their legs don't work right. Some are blind. Some are screaming at Jesus because they have evil spirits in them. Whatever is wrong, they know Jesus will heal them. And sure enough, when Jesus touches them or tells them to get well, they all get well again. Some have been sick for years and years and years. Now suddenly they are all right! You can see how happy they are.

SOME QUESTIONS TO ANSWER
1. Why are the sick people coming to Jesus?
2. Why are the people happy?

A LITTLE PRAYER
Thank you, Jesus, for making all those people well. Thank you for caring about how we feel.

A BIBLE VERSE FOR YOU TO SAY
When he spoke a single word, all the demons left. And all the sick

... were healed. MATTHEW 8:16

Jesus talks to his Father.
His Father is God above.
You, too, can talk to his Father—
He listens to you with love.

Jesus is praying. He is talking with God. You cannot see God in the picture, but he is there. God is listening. Jesus is thanking God and asking God to tell him what to do. We can pray too. We cannot see God, but we can thank him for our father and mother, and for our nice home, and for our friends. We can tell God we love him. God is always listening to us. He is glad when we talk with him. He wants to be our friend.

SOME QUESTIONS TO ANSWER
1. Where is God?
2. How can we talk to him?
3. Why should we talk to God?

A LITTLE PRAYER
Dear God, thank you that I can talk to you. Thank you for listening to me. Help me to listen to what you tell me.

A BIBLE VERSE FOR YOU TO SAY
Pray for each other. JAMES 5:16

The storm was wild, the waves were high, Disciples feared that they would die. But Jesus spoke, the wind stopped blowing, The boat arrived where it was going.

Jesus and his friends were in a boat going across the lake. Suddenly the wind began blowing angrily. It rained and rained and rained. Everyone was frightened except Jesus. He was tired, and he had gone to sleep in the back of the boat. Jesus' friends rushed to him and woke him up. "The boat is sinking," they screamed. "Everyone will die in the water." But Jesus is standing up. He tells the storm to go away. Immediately the wind stops blowing, and the waves disappear. The lake becomes smooth and safe again.

SOME QUESTIONS TO ANSWER
1. Why were Jesus' friends frightened?
2. Did the boat sink?
3. Why not?

A LITTLE PRAYER
How wonderful, Lord Jesus, that you can make the storms go away.

A BIBLE VERSE FOR YOU TO SAY
Why were you so afraid? Don't you have confidence in me yet? MARK

4:40

Jesus made the sick men well—
Count them, one to ten.
How many men said thank you?
Just one came back again.

Can you count the ten men? They were sick and sad. Then someone told them, "Jesus can make you well." So they asked Jesus to heal them. What do you think Jesus did? Did he give them some medicine? No, he just told the sickness to go away, and it did. Now the men are happy, because they are well again. But only one of the men has come back to thank Jesus! The others forgot. Do you ever forget to tell Jesus thank you? What should you thank him for? Well, he gave you a father and mother, and a home, and food, and many, many other good things. You can thank him for all these things.

SOME QUESTIONS TO ANSWER
1. What did all ten ask Jesus to do?
2. Why is the one man on the ground at Jesus' feet?
3. Did the other nine men say thank you?
4. Should you say thank you to Jesus? What are some things to thank him for?

A LITTLE PRAYER
Thank you, Jesus, for healing the ten men who were sick.
Thank you for all the kind things you do for me.

A BIBLE VERSE FOR YOU TO SAY
One of them came back to Jesus. . . . He thanked Jesus for what he

had done. LUKE 17:15-16

"Glory to God!" the people shout.
"Glory!" the children sing.
They wave the palms and spread their coats
To show he is their king!

All the people are very excited. They are thanking God because of Jesus. They are waving palm branches to show that Jesus is their new king. Some of them are taking off their coats and spreading them out like a carpet in front of him. They are doing this to show that Jesus is very great and good. They remember how he healed the people who were sick. They remember the little girl that Jesus brought back to life again. They remember the five thousand people Jesus fed with the little boy's lunch. No wonder they want Jesus to be their king! They do not know that Jesus will die for them.

SOME QUESTIONS TO ANSWER
1. Why are the people singing and putting their coats on the road?
2. What can we do to show Jesus that we love him?

A LITTLE PRAYER
Dear Jesus, thank you for being my great and good king. I want you to be in charge of my life.

A BIBLE VERSE FOR YOU TO SAY
God has given us a King!... Glory to God in the highest Heavens!

LUKE 19:38

Judas was Jesus' disciple, But Judas was sneaky and sly. He acted as if he loved Jesus, But really he hoped he would die.

The people wanted Jesus to be their king, but some of their leaders said no. The leaders decided to get Jesus killed. Judas, one of Jesus' disciples, said he would help them. He would take them to Jesus. Then they could arrest Jesus and take him away to die. Judas is kissing Jesus. He is just pretending to be Jesus' friend. The soldiers are going to tie Jesus up. Jesus could have asked God to send thousands of angels to help him, but Jesus didn't do this. He was willing to die because he loves us. He was willing to die to take away our sins.

SOME QUESTIONS TO ANSWER
1. What is the name of the disciple who helped Jesus' enemies?
2. Did Jesus ask God to send angels to help him?
3. Why not?

A LITTLE PRAYER
Jesus, I am sorry your friend turned against you. Help me never to turn against you.

A BIBLE VERSE FOR YOU TO SAY
He prayed, "My Father! . . . I want what you want. I will do your will,

not mine.” MATTHEW 26:39

How could you do it, Peter?
How could you hurt your friend?
Yet Jesus said, "I forgive you."
Even this sin he could mend.

Jesus told his disciples they would run away when soldiers came to get him. Peter said he would never, never do that. But Jesus said, "Tomorrow morning, before the rooster crows, you will say three times that you don't even know me." Sure enough, when soldiers came for Jesus, Peter ran away. He thought the soldiers might put him in jail. Someone asked, "Do you know Jesus?" "No!" he said. Someone else said, "Peter was with Jesus." "I was not," Peter said. A third person asked, "Is Jesus your friend?" Peter shouted, "Of course not! Quit bothering me!" Just then the rooster crowed. Peter is remembering what Jesus said. Now Peter is sorry. He does not think Jesus will forgive him. Peter is crying because of what he did.

SOME QUESTIONS TO ANSWER
1. What did Peter say he would never do?
2. Why did Peter say he didn't know Jesus?

A LITTLE PRAYER
Dear God, please help me never, ever, to turn against my friend Jesus like Peter did.

A BIBLE VERSE FOR YOU TO SAY
Satan has asked to have you.   But I have begged in prayer for you.

LUKE 22:31-32

Up there on the hill I see Jesus' cross, at Calvary. Jesus died for you and me. Jesus died to set us free.

They are killing Jesus. They have nailed him to a cross, and soon he will die. He is not dying because he was bad. Jesus never did anything wrong. He is dying because people are bad. He is dying because he loves us. He is dying for our sins. Some of the people are laughing. They are very, very cruel. They do not know Jesus is dying for them. How kind Jesus is to die for us. We should thank God every day because Jesus loves us and died for us.

SOME QUESTIONS TO ANSWER
1. What is happening to Jesus?
2. Who died for our sins?

A LITTLE PRAYER
Dear Jesus, thank you for dying for my sins. Help me to learn more and more about all you have done for me.

A BIBLE VERSE FOR YOU TO SAY
Truly, this was the Son of God! MARK 15:39

The night is past—
Look at the light!
Jesus is risen,
The world is bright!

After Jesus died, they put his body in a cave. Then they rolled a big stone across it so no one could get in or out. But look! The stone is rolled away! Jesus is outside! He is alive! This is his friend Mary Magdalene. She is so surprised! She was very sad because Jesus was dead. But here he is, alive again! God has brought him back to life so he can still be our friend. Jesus is telling Mary Magdalene not to be afraid. He is not a ghost. He is real! He is telling her to give the good news to his other friends. Jesus lives!

SOME QUESTIONS TO ANSWER
1. What wonderful thing happened to Jesus?
2. Who made him come back to life again?
3. What did Jesus tell Mary to do?

A LITTLE PRAYER
Thank you, Jesus, for dying for me. Thank you, God, for bringing Jesus back to life again. Thank you! Thank you! Thank you!

A BIBLE VERSE FOR YOU TO SAY
He has come back to life again. MATTHEW 28:6

They fished all night Without a bite, Till Jesus came And made things right.

Jesus' disciples were out on the lake fishing. They fished all night but couldn't catch a fish anywhere. Jesus called to them from the shore. "Any fish yet?" "No," they said, "not a bite." "Throw your nets on the other side of your boat," Jesus said. "Then you will have plenty of fish." So they did. Suddenly, there were so many fish in the net that they could not pull them into the boat! This wonderful miracle happened because the disciples did what Jesus told them to.

SOME QUESTIONS TO ANSWER
1. How many fish did the disciples catch all night?
2. What happened in the morning when they did what Jesus told them to?

A LITTLE PRAYER
Dear Jesus, help me to be like your disciples and do whatever you tell me to.

A BIBLE VERSE FOR YOU TO SAY
You are my friends if you obey me. JOHN 15:14

Jesus said, "For now, good-bye— I'm going home, but please don't cry. My Father's there, and angels too, And someday I'll come back for you."

One day Jesus was outside, talking to his disciples. Suddenly he began to float up into the sky! He disappeared into a cloud. As the disciples were staring in surprise, two angels came. They said, "Someday Jesus will come back again!" Where did Jesus go? He went to heaven to be with God, his father. When will Jesus come back? We do not know, but we must be ready to welcome him. Someday, maybe soon, he will return. Then we will see him and talk to him, just as the disciples did. We will be with him always.

SOME QUESTIONS TO ANSWER
1. Who told the disciples Jesus would come back again?
2. Where did Jesus go?
3. Will he come back again?

A LITTLE PRAYER
Dear Jesus, please come soon.

A BIBLE VERSE FOR YOU TO SAY
"Yes, I am coming soon!" *Amen!* *Come, Lord Jesus!* REVELATION 22:20

Jesus went away to heaven, And someday he'll return. Oh, the joys that we will have, The happy things we'll learn!

When Jesus comes back, it will be very exciting! Jesus will make everything good. We will never be unhappy or cry about anything again. Jesus knows our names. He will talk to us and take care of us. We will be with Jesus forever. While Jesus is away, he thinks about us every day. He thinks about how much he loves us. He thinks about how much he wants us to be with him. Someday we will! This is very good news for little people and big people. Jesus asks us to tell everybody the good news. He wants everyone to know he died for them. He wants everyone to know he is coming again. Will you tell people the good news?

SOME QUESTIONS TO ANSWER
1. Will Jesus come back again from heaven?
2. What does Jesus think about while he is away?
3. What is the good news that Jesus wants everybody to know?

A LITTLE PRAYER
Dear Jesus, we want to see you. We want to live with you. Thank you for loving us. Please come soon.

A BIBLE VERSE FOR YOU TO SAY
Jesus has gone to Heaven.   And someday he will come back again,

just as he went! ACTS 1:11

ABOUT THE AUTHOR

Kenneth N. Taylor is best known as the translator of *The Living Bible*, but his first renown was as a writer of children's books. Ken and his wife, Margaret, have ten children, and his early books were written for use in the family's daily devotions. The manuscripts were ready for publication only when they passed the scrutiny of those ten young critics! Those books, which have now been read to two generations of children around the world, include *The Bible in Pictures for Little Eyes* (Moody Press), *Stories for the Children's Hour* (Moody Press), and *The Living Bible Story Book* (Tyndale House). Now the Taylor children are all grown, so *Big Thoughts for Little People*, *Giant Steps for Little People*, *Wise Words for Little People*, and *Good News for Little People* are written with his twenty-seven grandchildren in mind.

Ken Taylor is a graduate of Wheaton College and Northern Baptist Seminary. He is the founder and chairman of Tyndale House Publishers. He and Margaret live in Wheaton, Illinois.

ABOUT THE ILLUSTRATOR

Nancy Munger, a free-lance illustrator, has prepared illustrations for many different media including textbooks, book jackets, album covers, magazine articles, and advertisements. Books she has illustrated include *The NIV Children's Bible* and *The Adventure Bible* as well as several other children's books. She also enjoys using her talents in her church. A board member of the church's childcare program, she helps to raise money for it by selling Christian children's prints.

Nancy is a graduate of Ferris State University and the Art Center College of Design. She and her husband, Doug Anderson, live with their two children, Jessie and Joshua, on a farm near Delton, Michigan, where they enjoy their many ponies, horses, sheep, goats, chickens, and ducks. About *Good News for Little People* Nancy says, "I treasure the time spent on this book because of the closeness I have felt to the Lord while working on it."